I0547401

PEACES

BY PATRICIA GARCIA

TO THE MOST HIGH

FOR CHET

TABLE OF CONTENTS

NOTE FROM THE AUTHOR

As part of my Native American heritage I tend to think of everything as medicine. I have often told people that my tarantula, One, is heart medicine. When I hold him I am filled with a powerful and primal force, sometimes resulting in the writing and singing of love songs. Once I was telling this to my cousin while she was reading a tarantula book. Afterward she read to me that the venom of the Chilean rose tarantula is considered to be a type of medicine for heart attack victims. One is a Chilean rose.

In a similar way I prescribe this book as a type of peace medicine. My greatest hope is that it will bring a sense of tranquility to your mind. While often achieving the desired effect I must warn you of possible (and reported) side effects. These include sadness and feeling like you want to cry. If you should experience these symptoms, consider putting this book down and picking up one by Thich Nhat Hanh. Either way I wish you peace, peace, peace.

SONGS

JAH HAS BEEN SO MERCIFUL
(Moscow, December 2002)

When I look at my life
I got everything I need
Don't suffer from fear
Or jealousy or greed

When I look at the world
It's beauty all around
From the ever-changing sky
To the ever-fruitful ground

When I look at my people
There's love in every heart
And that's just the beginning
That's just a part—of how

Jah has been so merciful to me
Jah has been so merciful to me
Sing with me and you'll feel it, too
Jah has been so merciful to you

When I look at my troubles from afar
I see them for the trivia that they are
I won't let them drown me, cos you see
Jah has been so merciful to me

When I look at war and chaos from afar
I see them for the life-size games they are
Some people love the struggle, you see
But Jah has been so merciful to me

Jah has been so merciful to me
Jah has been so merciful to me
When you accept no minus, only plus
You'll see
Jah has been so merciful to us

When I stop and look deep inside my soul
I see the universe as perfect and whole
Unconditional love feels all this space
Time to realize there's no better place

When I look at a big black dog
Prancing through white snow
And I feel his laughter
That's how I know, I know

Jah has been so merciful to me
Jah has been so merciful to me
Sing with me, that's how we discuss
Jah has been so merciful to us

Jah has been so merciful to me
Jah has been so merciful to me
Sing with me and you'll feel it, too
Jah has been so merciful to you

U CAN'T STOP THIS PARTY
(Amsterdam, 2003)

U can stop the rain
U can stop the pain
U can stop your brain
U can't stop this party

U can stop the hate
U can stop the wait
U can stop your fate
U can't stop this party

U can stop the crime
U can stop the time
U can stop your mind
U can't stop this party

U can stop the drugs
U can stop the hugs
U can stop your thugs
U can't stop this party

U can stop the jeers
U can stop the tears
U can stop your fears
U can't stop this party

U can stop the lying
U can stop the crying
U can stop denying
U can't stop this party

U can stop the truck
U can stop the buck
U can stop the fuck
U can't stop this party

U can stop the
U can stop the
U can stop the
U can't stop this party

IT
(Colorado, 2003)

Some say that it has all been said before
I say
No way

There are no problems
Only games we play
They begin and end again
My friend
Like Pac-Man

Hasn't all
It hasn't all been said
Hasn't all been said before
It

You and I have met before
When you and I were dinosaur
It happens just like this:
We meet I attack
We run you resist
In the end we kiss

Hasn't all
It hasn't all been said

Hasn't all been said before
It

You and I will meet again
When you and I are alien
It happens just like this:
We make love not war
We know what life is for
We live it all in bliss

Hasn't all
It hasn't all been said
Hasn't all been said before
It

There are no problems
Only games we play
They begin and end again
My friend
Like Tetris

NO LOVE LOST

No, I wouldn't say
Love can be just tossed away
Lost and stray—in the universe

No, I wouldn't say
Love cannot be bought
Lost is my purse—in the universe

Mind tallies how you bought and broke me
Heart calculates my cost
I add it all up
There is no love lost

There is no love lost
You're more valuable to me than you could
    ever earn

No, I wouldn't say
Love can be just thrown away
Lost in space—in the universe

No, I wouldn't say
Love cannot be bought, oh
Lost is my thought—in the universe

Mind tallies how I bargained for you
Heart calculates your cost
I add it all up
There is no love lost

There is no love lost
You're more valuable to me than you could
    ever learn

POETRY

NO MORE CONDITIONS
(California, Thanksgiving 2005)

No more conditions have to be met
Before I forgive those who have disrespected me
I forgive them

No more conditions have to be met
Before I forgive myself for the disrespect I've
    shown
I forgive I

No more conditions have to be met
Before I am at peace with the past
I am at peace with the past

No more conditions have to be met
Before I accept people as they are
I accept you

No more conditions have to be met
Before I see your light
For I see your light

No more conditions have to be met
Before I allow myself to feel loved
I am loved unconditionally

No more conditions have to be met
Before I feel truly thankful
And for that I am truly thankful

No more conditions have to be met
Before I accept change
I accept change preferably in quarters

No more conditions have to be met
Before I am able to let go of fear
I am letting fear go as I speak

No more conditions have to be met
Before I end the war within myself
You are witnessing the end

No more conditions have to be met
Before I can die satisfied
I am satisfied today

No more conditions have to be met
Before I can look myself in the eye and say it's
    all good
'Cause it's all good

No more conditions have to be met

Before I feel truly blessed
I am blessed by the most high, Jah Ras Tafari

No more conditions have to be met
Before I allow myself to be free
We are as free as we want to be

No more conditions have to be met
Before I do what I came here to do
I am doing it now

A BRICK TO THE HEAD
(California, December 2, 2005)

When I asked how you got your scar
You said someone threw a brick at your head
When I asked you why
You said you were young and couldn't
   remember

Well now I know why
Because you threw that brick at my head
As I fell to the ground it landed on my chest
Where it weighed heavily upon my heart

The brick was thrown out of fear
A continuation of chaos and confusion
A reactionary act of violence
To make one feel stronger and less vulnerable

Afterward I dreamt that I was lying in the earth
Dirt was being shoveled onto my back
I knew if I was going to protest that I must
   stand
But I decided just to stay there

However that was only a dream
And I am still alive

I take the brick from my body
It is not my load to carry

I choose not to throw this brick at you or
    anyone else
I place it on the ground and use it as a seat
When more bricks are thrown in my direction
I will use them to build a bench for meditation

Sitting near the ground
I bring stillness to my mind
Level vibrations surround me
The brick stops here

OBSERVATIONS OF A PEACEFUL MIND
(California, February 10, 2006)

TU HAIKU
(California, September 10, 2006)

Smiling as you came
Taking the seat behind mine
Was it on purpose?

Noticing you there
I cannot help but smile too
On purpose or no

PROSE

MY DOG DID MY HOMEWORK

Simon was sick and tired. Sick because he had a cold and sore throat, tired because his life was an unending cycle of school, work, and homework. As usual, Simon had gotten up at eight, made it to the university by nine (okay, nine fifteen), was in class until one, went to work at three, got off at eight, home at eight thirty, whew! He was tired. On top of everything his throat was sore, his nose runny, and the cold medicine made him sleepy and spacey.

All Simon wanted was rest. The problem was he had a creative writing project due in English—tomorrow. He had planned to start and finish it that night, not anticipating that he would feel so completely ill and unable. The project was to write a story from the point of view of someone completely different from oneself. The class had just read a short story written from the point of view of a young black teen written by a Latina woman. Now it was the students' turn to try their hands at this technique. Simon's last two projects were turned in late: this one had to be on time.

Normally enthusiastic about such a project, Simon simply didn't have the energy. On coming home he collapsed on the couch next to his four-month-old pug Bizkit. Bizkit sat upright, wagging his tail, smiling like only pugs do, hoping that now that Simon was home he would play. Simon lay face down on Bizkit's dog blanket showing no signs of play. Only Bizkit could fail to notice.

"Bizkit," Simon said raising his head, "Why can't we trade places for just the next eight hours? You write my story and I'll lay here on your blanket." Bizkit just looked at him with a look of happy non-understanding. Simon mumbled, "What am I going to do? I need to rest for a few minutes..." and with that he closed his eyes and fell asleep.

Worried over the project and sick as a dog, Simon dreamt that he and Bizkit really did trade responsibilities. Simon curled up on the blanket and slept. Bizkit jumped down from the couch, opened Simon's notebook on the coffee table, picked up a pen and began doing the creative writing assignment. "Good boy," Simon said snuggling deeper into Bizkit's blanket, as

Bizkit wrote page after page of the project, pen in paw, looking thoughtfully down at his work.

Simon slept late the next morning, glanced at his watch. "Shoot!" He grabbed his notebook and backpack and headed out the door. He was fifteen minutes late for English. One of the students was finishing reading his paper, written from the point of view of a Russian *babushka*. He finished in a Russian woman's accent, *"Spasiba, da svidaniya!"* The class applauded, the student bowed.

Then the professor turned to Simon, "Mr. Ellis, perhaps you will do us the honor of reading us your story?"

Simon gulped and stammered, "Um…um…"

"Or maybe you haven't completed the assignment, for the THIRD time in a row?" the professor remarked.

"No," Simon managed, "I have it," he said pulling the notebook from his backpack. He flipped through the pages until he came to the dog's writing. "Um," Simon began, "It's called...simply...*Woof.*" A few giggles were heard. "Here goes," Simon said lowly and began to read, "Woof woof, woof woof. Ruff ruff, woof woof woof. Grrrr...woof! Arf arf, woof woof..." The students erupted in laughter. "I'm sorry!" Simon tried to explain above their guffaws, "My dog did my homework!"

Simon awoke, sitting upright, sweating. It was just a dream! Thank god! What time was it? Five a.m. He still had time to do the assignment! Bizkit lay snoring softly beside him. "Bizkit," he whispered, "You've given me a great idea." And he sat down and wrote his assignment from the point of view of a dog--in English. Simon looked at the sleeping Bizkit and wrote about dog dreams: running freely in fields of green grass, finding a T-bone steak in the chow dish...

Bizkit lay sleeping soundly. His dreams were nothing like the dreams Simon wrote about. His mind never conjured up grassy fields or steak. Bizkit dreamt of images only found in an animal's imagination, like warm noises and gray scents. He dreamt of beautiful things,

things that find no expression in the written word.

MOSCOW IN SLIDES

Memories of Moscow flow back to me at unexpected times, for instance when I'm lying on an acupuncture table or cleaning the barbecue on a summer day. I experience them the way one might experience an LSD flashback: I'm not thinking of Russia or anything to do with that time zone when suddenly I'm thrown back to some moment I spent there. It's as if some mysterious spirit has dropped a slide into the projector of my daily perception. I see it all so clearly, every color and every visual detail of every building, every snowflake is exact. Other times I'll be reading literature in Cyrillic, but I won't be visualizing *Patriarshye* Ponds at all, instead I find myself walking under the streetlights of *Kravchenko* in snow.

These colorful flashbacks make me laugh because when a friend comes up to me and says, "So tell me about Russia," it seems that I am always at a loss for words. Where do I start? What aspect of the twenty months I spent there do I expound on? What song do they want to hear from all my records of

Russian study? The information my brain contains could fill Russian territory.

So here I present to you Dear Reader, Moscow the way I experience it, wherever I happen to be, in slides.

Slide: Explosion of light and shattering glass

I lived in an old Soviet style apartment. I slept in a Soviet style bed: a very thin mattress on top of divided sofa-type cushions with visible springs coming through. Hot water pipes in the bathroom doubled as clotheslines. And an old chandelier hung in the middle of the main room. Now here's what would happen: I would come home from an exhausting day of work and city life, flip the switch to the chandelier, and CHINK! Greeted by an explosion of glass and light. Then I would open my eyes to see smoke where one of the light bulbs had just exploded out of the chandelier. Broken light bulb glass could be found all over the room: beside the bed, various places on the rug and wooden floor, on the desk and chairs. After I cleaned up as much of the glass as I could find,

I would attempt to get the metal base of the light bulb out of the chandelier socket. I would stand on a chair with a cooking mitt on my hand, holding pliers, trying not to cut myself on broken glass, while loosening the metal from the socket. I was successful every time, but the last. It is still in there. And that is just part of the Russian experience: the lights don't just fizzle out quietly—they explode like gunfire.

Slide: Man wearing pants with hands in pockets

When you live in Moscow and travel on the metro (subway) you see homeless people everyday. Most of them just come and go from your vision and you're so used to it that you don't give it much thought. But once in a while you see a *bomzh* (bum) that leaves an impression on you. I saw one such man walking down *Svyetnoy Bulvar*. He was bald and completely naked except for a pair of old pants and a layer of dirt that covered his entire body. The trousers were too small for him, too short. There was no zipper in the fly and no buttons. The only things keeping the pants on his body were the two hands, which he kept in his pants pockets for this purpose. The passersby, including me, smiled because he looked quite comical, as if he were part of the circus that runs on that same boulevard. He didn't seem to mind—he seemed to be going somewhere.

Slide: People seated around long table set with food and bottles

The New Year celebration in Russia is a combination of Christmas, Halloween, and the 4th of July. It's like Christmas because of the decorated trees, the presents, and the feast. It's like Halloween because people wear funny hats and masks in the street. It's like the 4th because of all of the fireworks that begin several weeks in advance and culminate on the New Year itself. And, of course, it is like New Year's (staying up until midnight) and Chinese New Year (with animal emblems of whichever year is being welcomed). To bring in the Year of the Horse, *Galya* took me to an interesting New Year's party at her friend's house. The guests included professional musicians and singers so the entertainment was excellent. The majority of the partygoers were Russian and they found it very interesting that I had moved to Moscow to become more fluent in Russian. *Galya* told them that I sang and played a Russian song called *Milenkiti Moy* and they asked me to stand up and perform for them. I remember declining and feeling hesitant, I had never performed in front of a crowd that size, forget a foreign audience! However, everyone insisted and all the vodka I had consumed washed away some of my inhibitions. So I stood up in front of the room, of probably twenty some people, and started playing the Russian song on my little backpacker guitar, singing with my Californian accent. Nothing can describe the relief I felt, and the joy that enveloped me, when I realized other party guests knew the song I was playing. At first I heard the high pitched voices of a few older women singing. Then some male voices joined in. Until finally the entire room was singing! By song's end you couldn't even distinguish my voice from the others. It was a wonderful New Year's surprise.

Slide: Three neighbors in small elevator

As I was getting on the elevator of my apartment building one morning I was greeted by two of my neighbors, an attractive young man and woman. I mentioned that I was going to work and the man asked me if I was a journalist. I told him, no, that I was a teacher and a writer. He said, "Write this: Russians cannot find work in their own country." He went on to say that he and his wife used to go out looking for jobs, but now they just went out and drank vodka. Without thinking I laughed. With a straight face his wife kindly added, "It's true, now we just go drink vodka." I didn't know what to say, so I just said see you later and went to teach my class. About three hours later I returned to the apartment building. I was surprised to see the very same neighbors right next to the elevator. The woman was holding the man up against the wall, his eyelids were half-mast and it was clear he was incoherent. He was completely drunk. I offered his wife assistance. She refused and I noticed she was drunk, too: tears were streaming down her face and her hair was in disarray. "Don't mind us," she said to me, "this is how we are."

Slide: Big black cat on red Asian rug

My boyfriend had just helped me move into an old apartment building in the *Timiryazevskaya* region of Northern Moscow when we heard a cat meowing. We were surprised because my apartment was in a closed hall on the eighth floor. I walked into the kitchen to see a large black cat mewing at the window of the door that led to my balcony. We figured out that the cat must have crossed over from the neighboring terrace. I opened the door to let him in but the loud noise of the door frightened him and he speedily slunk back across the balcony division to his home. The next morning I awoke to the sound of the same loud mewing. "Oh," I said aloud rolling over in my bed, "kitty's on my balcony." As I was pulling off the covers to go let him in, you'll never guess what I saw: the black cat was sitting right in front of me on my living room rug! Meowing. I was astonished. I seriously wondered if I was dreaming. But it wasn't a dream: the cat had crossed over onto my balcony, jumped up, and pushed his way in through the *fortochka*, a small ventilation window. He is my real life

Begemot. His name is *Styopa* and I love him dearly.

Slide: Blond woman in blue dress at train station

I've heard train stations are notorious for the vagabonds that linger there. But nowhere have I seen so many as at *Leningradski Vokzal* (Leningrad Railway Station). One day I was heading there, I had just stepped out of the metro station next door, when I saw a blond woman in a blue dress lying on the ground. What struck me about her was that her hair was dyed crayon yellow and her dirty dress was electric blue, both unusually vibrant colors for a street person. There were other vagrants gathered speaking at her feet. But what didn't seem obvious, to anyone but me, was that this blond woman was dead. The soul had left the body. She was lying on the concrete with her hands above her head in a way that was very unnatural. The arms were completely too free. Something about those arms and her peaceful expression, entirely without motion, told me that she was not passed out and she was not asleep. I stared at her for a long, long time. Then I walked to the train station and took care of the business I had there. After some time I returned to the metro station, to the exit doors where I had seen the woman. I don't know why I went to the exit and not the entrance. Did I return to see her? Or had I just forgotten that the entrance was on the opposite side of the building, as on other occasions? I don't remember. What I saw when I returned was that the woman's body had been moved away from the metro doors and onto the plaza in front of the market. There was a homeless man mourning over her loudly, I think he was crying her name, kneeling and rocking with his live body over her lifeless one. Her blue-sleeved arms were still very freely thrown above her blond head.

Slide: Two people kissing in backseat of car

Galya, the owner of the first apartment I stayed at, had decided to ride with me to the airport. I was going home to America. The week prior I had spent in Czech Republic trying in vain to forget *Vova*, the young Russian I had fallen in love with. The night before I left Russia I spent drinking vodka into the wee morning hours with friends at Moscow State University. When I came back to the apartment *Galya* told me that *Vova* had been calling all night and that I must call him before I left. After short deliberation I called him and he came over at four in the morning, just in time to ride with us to the airport. Now, my American friend had told me that he could get me a taxi to the airport for fifty bucks. I later bartered with a taxi driver to take me there for twenty. When that driver failed to show up on time *Vova* found a taxi to take us to the airport for seven dollars, 200 rubles at that time, (a fact that *Galya* and I still talk about to this day!) On the ride to the airport, in the back of the cold dark taxi, *Vova* and I hardly spoke a word to one another. We held onto each other madly the entire way. I never embraced anyone so tightly. We kissed like two people who know they are never going to meet again.

BEE

(Remix 2006)

To the most high

The miracle is not walking on water but
walking on the Earth
-Master Linchi

1

Once upon a time there was a girl born into the
world. Her name was Bee. As a baby she cried
very hard and long, but as she grew she
stopped crying so much and became a normal
girl. She was a good student in class and she
loved to play tetherball. She was good at it, too.
Bee was pretty and sometimes when people
met her they thought, "That little girl is special
in some way."

It was true. Bee was special. She had felt it for
a long time. She didn't know how or why, but
she felt a little different from other kids and
even from the rest of her family. She wasn't

sure but she thought it might have to do with this one time she thought she was going to die.

Bee and her brother Simon were swimming in the ocean on a hot summer day. Bee had always loved the ocean and she usually swam deeper than the other kids. On this particular day she found herself deeper and farther away from shore than the others, farther away than she expected. She laughed to herself with some joy. But when she tried to swim back in, the waves began to carry her out further. Her arms became very tired. The other kids were playing and didn't notice she was gone.

Suddenly she could no longer keep her head above the waves. "Jesus," she said, "Help me, Jesus." And with that she went under, closing her eyes as she did. As she sank she thought about her mother and father, when all of a sudden she felt great warmth around her and two hands reached out and caught her. Bee opened her eyes to see Christ. He had a peaceful expression on his beautiful face as he said to her, "I'm here." That was all she saw before she lost consciousness.

When she came to, it was as if from sleep. She was lying on the seashore. No one noticed her until she opened her eyes. "Are you okay?" her brother asked, kneeling in the sand beside her.

"Yeah," she said, feeling perfectly fine.

"Come on," he said, running back into the shallow waves.

After that Bee's life went on as usual. She kicked everyone's ass at tetherball during recess. She studied in class and did her homework. After school she played games with Simon or by herself; she often played by herself. She had a good imagination.

Sometimes Bee would take some of her playthings into the large bathroom and lock the door. Then she would transform the bathroom into her own restaurant where she would serve imaginary customers. She would dress up in one of her mother's dresses, one from about fifteen years ago, and try to look like a waitress. Another one of her mother's dresses would be spread over the rectangular hamper as a flowered tablecloth. She used mismatched tea sets for dishes. The shower stall became the kitchen and the sink became the waitress' workstation. She used a Hello Kitty pen and the notepad some realtor had left on the doorstep to take orders from invisible customers who generally ordered soup and tea, both easily created from water.

2

One weekend their mother took Bee and Simon to the park to feed the ducks. She gave each of them half a loaf of bread in a plastic bag. As Bee and her brother approached the pond throwing bread, they were quickly surrounded by ducks, geese, and other birds. Bee climbed up and stood on a green wooden picnic table and attempted to distribute the bread in a democratic manner. She tried to throw far out to the small ducklings, while handing bread to the larger ducks and geese standing with her on the table; she wanted to reward them for their effort and bravery.

"Here's the last slice," Bee said, throwing a few pieces to some gold and black ducklings at the edge of the pond. With the last quarter of a slice in her hand she turned around and saw a large beautiful gander standing on the ground. He had black feet; feathers of various shades of white, brown, gray, and black; eye feathers that made him look as if he were wearing a mask; and an ebony beak.

"This is for you," she said, handing the unusual gander the last of her bread.

"Thank you," he said as he received the bread from her hand. Bee looked intently at the bird. Had he just spoken to her?

The other birds wandered away seeing that Bee was out of sustenance. Some of them wandered over to where Simon was still feeding the birds.

When the masked gander finished eating the bread he spoke to Bee: "Peace to you, Bee. I'm a messenger of god. You are, too. That's why you can understand me—to everyone else it just sounds like I'm quacking. Another messenger will contact you in the future, possibly with a task for you. Farewell." And with that the gander took off at a pace and gracefully flew to the center of the pond.

Bee stared after him in wonder and amazement, attempting to process what had just taken place. A goose had just spoken with her and told her that she was a messenger of god. That he was one, too. She would be asked to perform a task? Whoa. It was all very surprising.

Yet at the same time something about it made sense. Maybe this was why Bee had always felt different from the people around her. This could be why some people somehow sensed that she was special.

Bee watched the gander swim off in the direction of the sun.

3

Bee never told anyone about the goose or about being a messenger of god and all that. She had seen a guy on the TV news that said he was Christ and then killed a famous person. They had locked that guy up. Bee wanted to be free.

"Oh, no," Bee thought, "what if the task the goose was talking about is to kill someone?!" She didn't know if she could do it. She became worried. After a little while she remembered something her grandfather told her: "Worrying is the biggest waste of time. If people spent the time they spend worrying about things doing something they wouldn't have time to worry." She decided he was right and she stopped worrying about it. If god asked her to kill, she'd kill. She didn't want to fight with god.

Fortunately, god never asked Bee to kill. So far he hadn't asked anything of her. She attended to her everyday affairs as usual for many moons, never hearing a word from another messenger of god.

4

What happened next was a bit unpleasant for Bee and Simon: their parents got divorced. The kids would stay with their mother and see their father every other weekend.

Imagine a small house of three very sad people. Bee's mother hadn't wanted a divorce, but she couldn't handle a husband that came and went at will either. She didn't want that for herself or for her kids. She wanted someone stable like herself.

Bee was sad because she loved her father very much, maybe more than anyone in the world. She thought they had a special relationship. He gave her secret presents when Simon and her mother were not around. She always waited for him to come home from work around five, just as the sun was starting to disappear. After he left this became a particularly painful part of the day; she began to have a feeling of doom when the sun started to set, as if she was still waiting for him to come home, while knowing that he never was.

Maybe it hit Simon the hardest. His father had been his best friend, his role model, his ally in the household, his partner in crime. Now he was left behind with two females he found it difficult to relate to. It felt like a two against one situation. He felt very alone.

They all did.

But life goes on even for the lonely and broken hearted. Maybe especially for those...

Now that their mother had to work more often Simon and Bee became latchkey kids and spent a lot of time just with one another.

Simon began skateboarding. He was quite good because he wasn't afraid of falling down. When he got hurt he just got back on his board again. He would skate in the street in front of their house while Bee played handball with a rubber ball against the garage door, singing quietly to herself some tune she made up.

Of course, both of them were in school. Simon wasn't that interested in school, not like Bee. Bee excelled in every subject. It wasn't that she was naturally more intelligent, it was just that she had a lot of free time to do all of her assignments and she started learning things. She especially liked mathematics and art.

One Halloween Bee's class made jack-o-lantern masks from orange, black, and green construction paper. The students' names were written on the back of the masks, stapled to the wall, and each mask was given an identifying number. Bee's was 11. Next all the students voted by secret ballot on which mask was the best. Bee's mask took second place.

Bee began making more masks at home. At first she made full-face masks like the jack-o-lantern. She made a werewolf mask that Simon took a liking to and quickly made his own, wearing it in the dark hallway to scare the life out of his mother and sister. Eventually Bee started making more masks that only covered the top half of the face or just around the eyes.

Bee's mother thought that she had found a talent and took her to the craft store so that she could buy some serious supplies. There Bee saw stringed sequins that would be good for bordering eyes and thin green ribbon with purple ribbon roses at every inch or so that she thought would be a good way to tie a mask on. But there was one thing at the craft store that Bee absolutely had to have: feathers.

That same night Bee started her first feathered half mask. She used bright purple feathers and craft glue. Silver sequins outlined the eyes.

Small rows of faux flowers created unusual eyebrows. Two strings of purple ribbon roses would tie the mask to the head. The careful arrangement of feathers took her two nights to complete.

When it was all finished she wore it into the kitchen where her mother was making spaghetti sauce. "Bee that's beautiful! Where's my camera?" Bee wore a lukewarm smile, taking off the mask. "What's the matter, honey?" her mother asked.

"I don't know if I like it," Bee replied.

"Bee I think it's wonderful, but it's only your first one. If you're not happy with it, try again. You'll get it. All you have to do is believe that you are making the most beautiful mask in the world and you will do it. You're special, Bee," her mother said, stirring the spaghetti sauce and smiling peacefully to herself. Bee watched her cook.

"Do you like my spaghetti, Bee?"

"I love it," she nodded, eyes wide.

"When I cook it I imagine that I'm cooking for the king and queen," mother said, "You are the queen and Simon is the king of my world. And the spaghetti always turns out good. You two always have seconds!"

Half an hour later the three of them sat down to dinner. Mother's spaghetti was even better than usual that night, the garlic bread outstanding. Simon ate so much that he gave himself a stomachache. They all laughed about it, even Simon.

5

"The letter contained a declaration of love; it was tender, respectful, and copied word for word from a German novel."
-Pushkin, Queen of Spades

A few years went by and everything in the world got that much older.

Bee continued to study diligently and receive high marks. Simon continued to skate.

There was this one boy that Bee liked at school. He was a slim, good-looking Japanese boy, named Kahei. He had beautiful flawless light skin and jet-black hair and eyes. His hair was shaven underneath and in the back with longer hair on top that sometimes fell into his face, over his eyes. He was a younger than average smoker and in general he was labeled a troublemaker.

Bee had only a few friends at school, she tended to live in her own little world and spent much of her time outside of class alone. Oh, and Kahei had no idea that Bee was alive. Or maybe that's just how it felt to her.

Kahei was in Bee's art class. That is, when he wasn't ditching school or late (art was first period.) Kahei was an incredible artist. He always drew in black and white: black pen on white paper. "I'm pioneering the field of Biro art." Bee once heard him say.

"What the fuck is Biro, dude?" his friend laughed.

"Biro invented the ballpoint pen, fuckhead. It's one of the greatest inventions of all time. Show some respect."

Bee's heart beat fast inside her chest as she overheard this. She looked at the ballpoint pen in her hand and fell suddenly in love with it.

Sometimes she would catch glimpses of Kahei's drawings: sleek, smart, robot men in hand to hand combat, marching in armies, fighting for freedom. Their metal bodies were composed of perfect geometric shapes. He created the perfect illusion of their eyes glowing. They had no other facial features. They, too, were flawless.

One week Kahei didn't come to school. He had been suspended. Bee heard two rumors about why. One said that he had told the science teacher to go fuck himself. Another said that he had brought some type of explosive to school. Either story could have been true. He might have even done both.

When he returned to school the edges of the long part of his hair were bleached white. Bee secretly drew Biro sketches of his new look. No one else their age had changed the color of their hair. He broke every rule.

One day Bee was sitting on a low brick wall outside the liquor store, waiting for Simon who was still inside buying candy. She was eating a Big Stick Popsicle when she saw Kahei and another kid with him walking toward the liquor store, about to walk by where she was sitting. She pretended not to notice. Kahei had an unlit cigarette hanging from the corner of his mouth. As the two of them passed, Kahei leaned toward Bee and asked, "Got a light?" Then he smiled and laughed, walking on, not waiting for an answer. His friend laughed, too.

Bee watched him walk away, her heart racing: he had never spoken to her before. He had smiled in her direction. She replayed the incident in her mind. Red drops of juice fell from her ignored Popsicle onto her white shorts and her leg.

6

The next year Kahei was transferred to another school for reasons of his behavior. It would be many years before Bee heard his name again.

7

More years passed. Summers. Winters.

One fall Bee sat making masks for Halloween as was her custom. She was making one now of black feathers. Red sequins surrounded the eyes. White feathers came down from the outer corners of the eyes, spread out and down until they shot off the mask. The white feathers would end in a light curl on the cheeks of the masquerader.

On that particular autumn evening, Bee's mother had one of her good friends over. Her name was Josephina. She was a journalist.

Since they had a guest mother prepared a special supper: homemade lasagna accompanied by zucchini and tomatoes. Need I say more? It was delicious. Simon was out with friends so the three ladies sat down to eat. During the course of dinner Josephina took an interest in the attractive young person who was Bee.

"Your mother tells me you're a talented artist, Bee. What kind of art do you do?"

"I make masks," she replied.

"Halloween masks?" Josephina asked.

"Well, masks for everything, for Mardi Gras, for parties, for Halloween."

"They're feathered masks," mother added, "They're very expressive. I think Bee must have been a bird in a past life."

"Are you working on anything at the moment?" Josephina asked.

"Yeah," Bee replied, "I finished one before dinner. I can show it to you later if you're interested."

"I'm very interested. Please do."

After supper, mother prepared hot chocolate. While it cooled Bee ran to her room to get the mask. At her desk she checked to see if the glue was dry: not quite. She decided to show Josephina a different mask that didn't have wet glue. The one she chose was her mother's favorite: it was white, gray, brown, and black with wild striped and spotted feathers shooting up and down from the corners of the mask. When Bee put the mask on she felt like a wild bird, maybe because she looked like one, maybe because she was.

With the mask on and her long wavy hair curling up at the ends Bee walked into the kitchen where mother and Josephina still sat speaking. Josephina stopped mid-sentence when she saw Bee walk in.

"The one I'm working on isn't dry yet. So this is a different one," Bee was saying.

"This one's my favorite," her mother said smiling at her daughter and the impression she was making on their guest.

"Oh, my god," Josephina said in amazement, "That's a real work of art, Bee. Would you mind if I got my camera and took a few pictures of you?"

"Okay," Bee shrugged.

8

As I've already mentioned Josephina was a journalist. She covered world news. One of her boyfriends, however, covered local news. When Josephina saw Bee in her mask she thought *this kid is news.*

That night Josephina took several pictures of Bee in her wild bird mask at her desk where the black feathered mask stood drying. She said that she wanted to take the pictures to show her friend Miguel who covered local news. If he liked the pictures and masks he may come to take more photos and interview Bee; would that be alright? Sure, it sounded interesting. By that age Bee was already used to people looking at her and wanting her picture. Something about her seemed to draw people's attention.

And sure enough Miguel was no exception. He fell in love with Bee and her masks. He took several more photographs of her wearing various masks in her room and outside in the sunlight.

He interviewed her and wrote an article about her that was featured on the front page of the local news section of the newspaper. There was even a tiny picture of Bee on the top banner of the front page of the paper showing that her story was inside. The caption read: 'Beauty of life' inspires young mask maker, D-1.

9

Bee became somewhat of a local celebrity and everyone wanted one of her masks. She sold dozens and put some of the money into making more.

Her proud parents showed the newspaper to all their friends. One of her father's friends was a commercial photographer. He told Bee's father that she should be a model and that he'd like to take some pictures of her. Her father agreed that his daughter should be a model and told his friend Carlo that he'd ask her about it.

Bee was interested in modeling, too. She used to collect pictures of her favorite models like Kees Poort. She dreamed of doing a photo shoot with Kees. And being in front of the camera was just another outlet for her creative expression.

Bee's father took her to a practice photo session at Carlo's studio and the results were remarkable. The combination of Carlo's talent in photography and Bee's natural gift for modeling produced a perfect match.

Later when Carlo received an assignment to photograph a line of Italian women's shoes he immediately thought of Bee and ordered all the shoes in a small size to fit her feet. The ad campaign was smashing and sexy. The shoe company was very pleased with the results. Carlo even gave her a pair of shoes from the shoot, the pair he knew to be her favorite.

The next shoot they did together was for some wild bikinis from California. Bee's father was again present to supervise the photo session. He felt a bit strange watching his young daughter doing some pretty risqué poses in a very small bikini, but he could appreciate her gift. She was an absolute natural. Carlo gave her hardly any direction, all that he was saying between camera clicks was, "Wow... yeah... good..."

The bikini ad campaign was a huge success for everyone involved. Bee even saw one of the ads in a major fashion magazine. She saved the magazine.

10

As Bee grew older she developed many talents. She still excelled in school. She wasn't at the very top of her class because it just wasn't that important to her. She worked hard at her studies because Bee worked hard at whatever it was she felt she had to do. From her grades it was clear that she would have her choice between several major universities.

She had also become quite a cook. Well, Bee's mother's father was a professional chef, and

Bee's mother was a great cook as well. Her mother taught Bee and she also learned from her example. She made an excellent lasagna, delicious fresh herb marinara sauce, and killer soups. She loved to make hot foods. One of her specialties was a salsa recipe that had been handed down from her father's mother to her. If you ate enough of it you would cry when you ate it.

And there was another thing that Bee had a great talent for: arranging fruit. Yeah, I suppose some might consider it an unusual gift, but it was an evident one in Bee. It didn't matter if you gave her five oranges and one green apple she would make it look like a masterpiece. She instinctively knew the angle that every pomegranate should be placed at in relation to every thin-skinned lemon. She knew how a stem should curve and the way to display the skin in its most appealing light. Whenever Bee arranged a bowl of fruit someone would walk by and say, "Somebody should paint that."

Of course, you shouldn't believe that everything Bee touched turned to gold. That wasn't how it was. She had her faults just as we all do. She often trusted people that others did not trust. She sometimes loved people that seemed incapable of love. She had a strange taste in males. She would get totally sprung on some physically attractive jerk that didn't care whether she lived or died, dreaming about him for years at a time. She would sometimes hold negative feelings inside until it made her physically ill. She didn't always show the proper respect for herself. On occasion she broke hearts.

But no one is perfect in this imperfect world. Or maybe I should say that what makes this world so complete is that everyone is precisely who they need to be.

11

The bikini company liked Carlo's photos of Bee and they asked him to do another photo shoot with her in a tropical location: Costa Rica. Carlo and Bee were excited about the shoot and going to Costa Rica. Bee's father would accompany them.

The three of them stayed in a very nice hotel in the capital, San Jose. The day after they arrived, Carlo and Bee took a bus away from the capital to a smaller village where they could do the photos capturing the beauty of the land. Bee's father had to stay behind because the airport had lost his luggage and he had to go back to the airport to locate and retrieve it. They all agreed to meet back at the hotel in time for supper.

The bus ride into the countryside took three hours up a windy, mountainous road. Carlo and Bee looked out the window the entire time taking it all in. They both felt some motion sickness and a girl next to them was ill. Bee felt like vomiting, too, but it remained only a feeling. She probably would have been sick, but she was sort of confined to her seat on the bus. She felt as if she would feel better if she could just vomit and get it over with. She was reminded of something she read about a Native American ceremony: one must get sick before one is well. Bee thought that was the truth.

When they finally reached their destination they discovered that they were in paradise.

Everywhere was green with a river or stream running through it. The songs and calls of exotic birds and animals played like a soundtrack to life. The people were kind and beautiful. Bee thought, "God lives here."

Although they both felt queasy from the bus ride they were inspired by their surroundings and quickly set off to work. They found an ideal location in a crystal clear stream that ran through gorgeous green trees and plants, at its source two waterfalls poured into it like two maidens almost facing one another, emptying large, bottomless jugs of water from the top of a cliff.

Towards the end of the session a light rain started to fall. Carlo continued taking pictures of Bee as the rain wet her hair and body; she looked quite striking, like a wild animal that accepts rain just as it accepts sunshine. When the rain began to pour and storm they had to quit for the camera equipment's sake.

With the coming of the rainstorm they decided to stay the night in the village where they were. Neither one of them liked the idea of riding the bus in a tropical rainstorm; the tight turns on high cliffs had seemed sketchy enough on a dry road under the sun. They didn't want to take too many chances.

That night Carlo and Bee dined at a seafood restaurant. They toasted to the success of the photo shoot with a shot of guaro. They rented a room with two beds across from the restaurant from the restaurant owner. There they smoked some really pleasant chronic and drank some more guaro.

Soon Bee was feeling super. Out of this world, you might say. So good in fact that when Carlo asked her to dance to the music they could hear from the disco close by, she danced with her body pressed against his. And when he began to unbutton the top of her shirt and feel her taut breasts, she melted in his arms. At the time she didn't realize he had drugged her drink with GHB. Needless to say, she wasn't very coherent...

After Carlo had her completely naked he touched her all over her tanned slim body. When she started to wilt he took her in his arms and carried her to the bed. As she passed out Bee prayed silently in her head, "Jesus, I'm in your hands." She felt his presence and her mind went black.

12

The next day Bee was violently ill. Carlo explained it away to Bee's father as food poisoning from the restaurant and mentioned that she had had a few drinks, too. Bee was mystified by the color of her vomit. She asked Carlo, "Why is it purple?" He just shrugged.

Bee felt like dying that day and in the weeks ahead her soul felt disturbed and sick. She couldn't remember what happened that night (GHB can give you amnesia), but she knew something was definitely wrong.

As weeks passed memories from that night came back to her one by one. And she began to realize what had happened. She had not voluntarily consumed anything that would make her vomit the dark pinkish purple it was and she had never desired sexual relations with Carlo.

Bee told the police what had happened but there wasn't anything that they could do without any evidence. The drug was no longer in her system. It had given her amnesia. There was nothing except Bee's returning memory of the truth.

Bee decided to leave the case to a higher court, the court of god. She knew he would take care of things. Bee believed in karma: what you do comes back to you. As ye sow so shall ye reap. She tried to comfort the pain with these thoughts.

Even though, the next several months were very difficult for her. She dreamed of revenge. She beat herself up for her part in it. Many nights she cried herself to sleep. Day and night the horrors of the event replayed themselves in her mind.

One time she felt so saddened and ashamed she thought that she was supposed to die. One night she ate a lot of ganja food, more than she knew was good for her. But she just didn't care. She was tired of walking around, dead inside from what happened, like some type of zombie. So she ate the ganja food at this party, hung out for awhile, and passed out for a time in an armchair. When she awoke it was very early in the morning. She wandered the streets a bit, but she was finding it very hard to walk and stay standing.

There was a house for sale in the neighborhood where Bee was walking. It looked vacant, the grass was overgrown and dandelions formed a wild garden. Bee knew she couldn't walk much farther, so she went to the side of this house and lay down in the tall grass. She laughed a little at herself as she looked up at the sky.

"Here I am, god. Please take me," she thought, looking at a dandelion and hallucinating.

"Not yet, Bee," came a wordless answer from deep within her being. Bee could feel it was some type of spirit speaking through her, to her. "There's more for you to do."

"Okay," Bee consented with hot tears filling up her eyes, overwhelmed by the thought of going on, "Okay, god, I'll do it for you," she said, crying.

She lay there for a long while hallucinating and crying. Morning came and she could hear people in the house next door in their kitchen, cooking breakfast.

Suddenly Bee heard something in the grass near her. She turned her head to see a black cat. It looked at her with yellow eyes. "Kitty," Bee whispered in her stupor. The cat came close and examined Bee's head and face with its nose and eyes. Bee remained very still so as not to scare it.

Then the cat began to lick Bee's face where her tears had fallen and half-dried. "Oooh," Bee smiled and moaned.

As the cat licked her face it began purring, but it wasn't just an ordinary purr, it was saying something. Somehow Bee could understand what it was purring and softly mewing, even though it wasn't anything close to English or regular words. The cat said, "I'm one, too. I have a message for you: forgive him. Forgive yourself. And you'll be free."

"Thank you," Bee went to speak, but somehow mewed instead.

"Don't mention it," was purred back with a lick on the nose and then the cat was off as quickly as it had appeared.

Bee lay there a long time thinking about that.

13

Simon had a very sweet girlfriend. She was good to the people around her. I guess you could say that she was a little like Bee's mother. And she and Bee were friends.

Bee herself didn't have a boyfriend. Well, not in the traditional sense.

She fell in love with a charming, attractive young man she met at a concert. He was an interesting and talented artist. He was very attracted to Bee who was quite beautiful, like a wild flower or a dandelion. The young man felt strong sexual desire for Bee. Later, he felt another strong emotion for her that he didn't completely understand. Unfortunately, it made him rather uncomfortable and he shied away from Bee without any kind of explanation.

She was often attracted to troublemakers. One guy she dated went to prison under mysterious circumstances. What Bee saw in these guys is hard to say, but what I think it was, was that she thought their wildness was freedom like her own. Later, she would learn that it was quite the opposite thing: it was irresponsibility and destructiveness. But Bee was young; she'd figure it out in time.

After heartache and disappointment Bee decided to try something different. She created an imaginary boyfriend. She didn't have a name for him; she simply called him her imaginary. He was physically striking, erotic, a little exotic, interesting, a good conversationalist, respectful, free... In short, he was a lot like Bee. He was a singer.

14

One day Bee's mother showed her a newspaper clipping. A young man in their area, about Bee's age, had been playing a game of Russian roulette with his brother and a friend, when he shot and killed himself. It was Kahei.

15

The next day Bee was feeling down. Sometimes when she thought too much about things she became depressed. Today it seemed that negative thought after negative thought was springing up in her mind.

"Stop!" she said to her brain out loud, as she stopped and stood still for a moment. "Maybe I'm just dehydrated," she thought, walking to the kitchen, "Maybe I need to eat; nutrients."

She poured herself a large glass of room-temperature drinking water then pulled a package of noodle soup from the pantry. She put two cups of water on the stove to boil and began looking at the package of soup. It was red and white with a picture of the soup on the cover. Pretty Korean characters gave cooking instructions and labeled what was inside.

"Beautiful letters," Bee said, "I wonder what it says..." She continued studying the package.

Suddenly an invisible switch flipped on in Bee's head and all of a sudden the Korean writing became coherent. She couldn't believe her eyes. The package read, "FLAVORFUL BROTH! DO NOT REFRIGERATE," then in bright green letters it read, "ENTER THE CONTEST: SAVE THE WORLD".

That was a little strange she thought, "What contest?" But as soon as she flipped the package over, it all became incoherent again, and Bee was left puzzling over the series of small pictures that in Korea were letters.

"Whoa," Bee said and set the package down on the counter. That was mysterious. The words ENTER THE CONTEST replayed themselves in her mind.

The water began to boil and Bee put the noodles in it.

16

A few days later Bee was lying down on her bed in the middle of the afternoon. She had just finished meditating and she felt relaxed. Warm sunshine heated the room and Bee's body. It felt good.

As Bee nestled her head into the pillow she saw her cell phone on the nightstand. I guess I should explain that this particular cell phone was only a cell phone by appearance. In actuality it was a handheld video game on which you could play one of twenty-five versions of Tetris. But Bee, being who she was, often used this toy to pretend she was talking to someone on the phone. Now she decided to call her imaginary.

They exchanged hellos. He was at home. They began having phone sex. Bee got excited listening to his uneven breathing over the line; he was getting off.

When they finished they were both getting tired and were getting off the phone when the imaginary said, "Think about entering the contest, Bee."

"What contest?!" Bee asked perplexed. Her imaginary just laughed, gave her an over-the-phone kiss, and hung up.

"What fucking contest?" Bee mumbled as she put the phone down and dozed off in the afternoon sun.

17

She was asleep for about thirty minutes when the phone rang: the real phone. It was Bee's friend, Jim.

"Hey, Bee, they're having a cooking contest down here at the hotel. Have you heard about it?"

"Yes," Bee said, a little out of it, "No. Kind of."

"Oka-a-ay," Jim said a bit confused, "Did I wake you?"

"Yeah, it's alright though. Tell me about the contest."

Jim told Bee that the contest would be in a month at the hotel downtown. It sounded like a big deal, cooks would be coming from all over to participate, and two finalists would be chosen to have a cook-off on television. You didn't need to be a certified chef to compete; all you needed was an original recipe and the entry fee. The grand prize was $5000.

"Sign me up," Bee told Jim.

18

What happened next couldn't have been predicted. Or maybe it could have. Maybe it had all been mapped out long ago and everyone was just following some invisible charted course. In any case, here's what happened.

Jim, Simon, and Bee all went to a concert. It was one of their very favorite bands—119. They sang and danced to every song. They were on the floor.

During a song called "Dutiful Master" Bee noticed an attractive young man who was dancing close by. He seemed to be glancing over at her occasionally. That was okay with her 'cause honey was fine: he was slim with dark toned skin and black curly hair. Bee couldn't help but smile as she looked at him; he was so pleasing to the eye.

When 119 started playing "All Fixed Up" Jim, Simon, and Bee went crazy, this was one of the songs they loved most. When the lead singer, Tick, sang, "You've got to let go of fear/ And hold on to respect..." Bee screamed with delight. She caught Tick's attention and they made eye contact for a brief moment.

Near the end of the show the band played a song called "Who Cooked the Herb?" Jim lit up a fat chronic joint he had brought for this specific purpose. As Bee was dancing to the tune she felt someone touch her arm. She looked over to see the dark curly haired boy. He was offering her a lit joint and exhaling smoke into the air then he simply smiled. Bee accepted the offering and it turned out to be very high quality.

The boy danced near Bee until the end of the show. When the concert was over Bee learned that his name was Dmitri. He asked her if he could take her out sometime. She told him yes. They exchanged phone numbers and hugged goodbye. As he embraced her he kissed her lightly on the cheek.

The next day he called her and they went out that night. Dmitri took Bee to a dark, small Mexican food restaurant that wasn't in the best part of town. All the employees there were Latinos and you could here Spanish coming from the kitchen.

Bee was starving and she salivated as she scanned the menu. She decided on the chile relleno. Bee was very surprised that when the waitress took her order Bee ordered in Spanish which she had never spoken more than a few words in her life:

"Me trae un chile relleno. Quiero unos frijoles refritos. Y trae una botella de agua, por favor."

When the waitress walked away Dmitri asked, "You speak Spanish?"

"Uh... sometimes... I guess," Bee managed through surprised laughter. She was laughing not only at her unexpected talent, but because Dmitri was smiling and it seemed to fill her with joy.

It was some of the best Mexican food she had ever tasted. Dmitri said that it was his favorite restaurant and he was pleased that Bee enjoyed it.

After dinner the two took a drive along the beach and talked. It seemed like they talked about everything: they talked about music, both of them loved reggae, they both loved 2pac; they talked about their families, they were both close with theirs; they talked about spirituality, both believed in god, karma, reincarnation...

After a while they parked and walked down a long cement staircase to the beach. On the beach Dmitri told Bee that he was moving soon to go work in another state. He said that it was too bad that he and Bee hadn't met earlier. Bee agreed; it seemed like they could be friends. Dmitri kissed Bee. As they walked along the beach he held her hand. It was a lovely evening: the sky was cloudless and deep blue, the moon glowed bright white, illuminating everything below, emulating the sun.

The new friends drove home, parted, and promised to meet again soon.

Dmitri called Bee a few days later and invited her over to his house for dinner and a dip in the hot tub. Bee accepted and they met around eight that night.

Bee was very excited to learn that Dmitri was making tostadas for dinner. She spoke with him in the kitchen as he prepared the food. Dinner was delicious. Afterwards they smoked a joint in Dmitri's room and started kissing. Then Dmitri suggested they go out to the hot tub. That sounded good to her so she got into her bikini, he got into shorts, and they went out back with the CD player, some CD's, some smoke, and some drinks.

They had a great time in the hot tub, listening to Steel Pulse, talking about places they'd been and things they'd done. Bee told Dmitri of the time she met Haile Selassie I at Reggae Room. They talked about the future, what they wanted to accomplish in life! Then for a few minutes they were quiet. They sat back, relaxed, and took in the stars. When the hot tub got too hot they jumped in the pool. And then back in the hot tub.

That night they had out-of-this-world sex and Dmitri fell asleep with his arm around Bee. Bee didn't fall asleep until early morning. The intense beating of her heart kept her awake.

19

Dmitri moved a few days later. He promised to write.

Bee was sad that she had just met a really cool person and he was going, but she was also busy—she needed to come up with a flavorful recipe for the cooking contest.

20

Bee had dozens of recipes to choose from. There was a red and orange salad she created with nectarines, red grapes, red apple, mandarin oranges, raspberries, etc. There were peanut butter and vanilla cookies; and portobello mushroom and pineapple shish kabobs. There was even an interesting dish called whipped cream soup, topped with whipped cream and a fresh cherry. But none of these recipes seemed right for the contest. Well, not to Bee.

Should she go with something tried and true or should she go out on a limb? It wasn't a question she thought about for long: something in her soul drove her to create something that no one had ever even dreamed of before.

She thought about it for days: whenever her mind veered into unproductive thought, she would bring her concentration back: what could she contribute that would really say Bee? What did she have to give to the world?

Noodles kept coming to mind. Pasta. Some type of special sauce... a dark sauce or soup? For days, ingredients danced around in her head: honey, miso, lemon... Should it be buttery or sweet? Spicy or sour? Should she use star pasta or linguini?

All of this rolled around in her head between daily tasks and meditation. And just when she thought she had it, something wouldn't seem quite right. She would then step back, look at the complete picture, figure out what wasn't working, and change it.

In the end Bee came up with a complimentary combination. It was something different and fresh, the ingredients melded together in such a way that when one tasted them they were somehow soothed by their harmony.

21

Jim accompanied Bee on the day of the big contest. Nervous and excited chefs worked busily at their workstations. Bee felt a little intimidated by the fact that all of the other chefs seemed older than she was, but what did that really matter? She reminded herself that she'd been creating recipes since she was a small child-- since she could remember. Some people were just born to do what they do. And overall Bee felt a rush of enthusiasm from being around her colleagues and all of that creative energy.

Bee set to work on her masterpiece. She snapped a few handfuls of rotini pasta in half and added it to boiling water. She created a dark sauce from water, unsweetened cocoa, and the slightest bit of hot Chinese mustard. She cut golden plantains into French-cut rounds and fried them. She put the sauce on the bottom of an ivory pasta dish and lined one half of the plate with the plantains, one half with a layer of pasta. Next she drizzled a zigzag of dark cocoa sauce over everything, followed by a zigzag drizzle of honey over everything, and garnished the meal with fresh honeysuckle. And there it was: Noodles Beestyle.

The chef to the right of Bee couldn't help but notice the unusual cook to her left. Her name was Olga. She liked Bee's style. She was getting ready to open a restaurant downtown. Olga gave Bee her card and told her that she was looking for original chefs like Bee for her new restaurant. Olga had a beautiful business card with a watermark. She also had a very good energy about her. Bee told her that she would call her.

When all was said and done the contest judges chose two finalists for the televised cook-off for first place. The first one was a man who had cooked a turkey dish with vodka cream sauce and mashed potatoes. The second finalist was a woman who prepared a colorful vegan chow mien with fried tofu.

22

"Jah Love will carry I home."
-Steel Pulse, Babylon Makes the Rules

Back home, late at night, Bee entered a long meditation.

She went to the back of the house, the quietest part, went into the bathroom and closed the door. She turned on the light, opened a drawer, pulled out a box of matches, lit a candle, and turned the light off.

She positioned a small wooden stepping stool on the opposite wall from the shower. As she arranged the room she took deep breaths, saying in her head, "Taking in oxygen, taking in positivity." As she breathed out she thought, "Letting go of carbon dioxide, letting go of negative feelings and vibrations, letting go of negative energy."

She sat straightly on the stool facing the shower curtain. The curtain was clear and directly in her line of vision stood a dark blue shampoo bottle. She rested her eyes on the bottle and focused her visual attention there. For the next 20 minutes or so her eyes wouldn't leave the bottle except to blink.

Next she began to clear her mind. She began to let go of all the thoughts running through her head. When the thought came into her mind that she had left some food in the car she told herself that yes, she needed to bring it in: she would automatically remember to do it when she was done with this. Then she continued to clear her mind: she visualized a clear rectangular plastic button on which was etched the word CLEAR in capital letters. She pushed this button in her mind's eye and thoughts cleared away. When good thoughts of the contest and being with Jim that day entered her mind she smiled and thought to herself, "You have plenty of time to think about that later," and then she pressed the CLEAR button and sent them away.

Once she had cleared her mind as much as she could she sat silently in the peace of that clarity. After a few minutes passed she began to give thanks to the most high: Dear god, thank you for the unconditional love of the universe that constantly surrounds me. Thank you for my mother, for her example and her guidance, for the security she provides me. Thank you for my father, my brother, my family, and all of my friends. Thank you for Jim who has taught me to laugh and who reminds me to keep a sense of humor in all situations. Thank you for Rohan who taught me that life is a party and to never stop celebrating no matter what challenges arise. Thank you for my imaginary, my spirit guide, who teaches me how to be.

Thank you for giving me a warm bed to sleep in at night and in the day. Thank you for giving me food to eat when I'm hungry. Thank you for my clothes and shoes and for the fact that I never need to go cold.

Thank you for my dog, Quixote, who teaches me that the sweetest love is unconditional.

Thank you for my health, for the fact that I can breathe, walk, run, dance and sing freely. Thank you for the venereal disease that guy gave me; at the time it was so painful, but now I understand that illnesses and mental anguish can be used as springboards for spiritual growth.

Thank you for everything good and bad that has happened to me, it's made me who I am today.

And on that note she pushed the CLEAR button and sat quietly in her mind's peace. Still concentrating on the dark blue shampoo bottle she began to hallucinate softly. She saw iridescent colors and the clear shower curtain appeared to be waving like liquid, noiselessly. She watched, enjoying the show.

While her visual concentration rested on the bottle, her mental concentration centered on the center of her forehead, right above the eyebrows. She focused this third eye with her other eyes on the shampoo bottle.

When outside thoughts tried to enter her space she no longer pushed the CLEAR button, but instead said in her head the word peace. Peace... peace... peace... peace... peace... And thoughts fell away.

Her mind reached a deeper peace, but slowly began to wonder again. She then turned her thoughts to forgiveness. In her mind she said I forgive Dmitri for saying he was going to call and never calling. It's possible he had other important things to do.

I forgive my father for leaving our family. His life's path needed to take another direction for some reason. I'm certain of that.

I forgive Carlo for drugging and molesting me. It wasn't personal. All he really wants is love just like everyone else. Someone probably made him feel powerless once and now he's trying to regain that power. At any rate I wish him no harm. I wish him well.

And most of all I forgive myself for mistakes I made, traps I stepped into, some traps I helped set. I forgive myself and recognize that it was all done in the name of experience.

She then began to clear her mind again, this time repeating the word respect. Respect... respect... respect... respect... respect... And this came into her mind: respect every individual and every spirit for its contribution to the universe. All are necessary. All serve one.

Then came a long period of silence. She felt bliss there.

In the end she came back down to earth, listening to the sound of her heart, it beat: be... be... be... be...be...

23

'U can stop the rain
U can stop the pain
U can stop your brain
U can't stop this party'

The following weekend was Josephina's wedding. You may recall that Josephina was the journalist friend of Bee's mother. Josephina had also become Bee's friend and even asked her to make the wedding favors that each guest would receive at the reception.

Bee and her mother worked diligently to make one hundred masquerade masks that would cover the eyes of the guests. On one edge or another of each mask Bee's mother wrote in a lovely script, "Josephina & Miguel Forever." Bee decorated each mask a variety of ways, using various types of feathers: some had feathers that gave the masquerader eyebrows; others had feathers that shot up from the outer corners of the eyes. The feathers were of many different colors. In the end, no two masks were alike.

Bee and her mother attended the wedding ceremony, which was in a park.

Bee's mother looked radiant that day. It wasn't what she was wearing, although that was also very nice and neat; it was the good energy that was spread by her bright wide eyes and happy smile. When Bee looked at her it was as if she could see the spirit of a young woman her own age, playing out the best days of her life. She was a beautiful animal in the sunshine.

The setting was very peaceful and pleasant on lush green grass near a large pond. Large groups of family members and good friends gathered for both bride and groom. Birds sang in the sky.

A musician in hemp and sunglasses began playing the wedding march on synthesizer and Josephina appeared from the back of a white van, looking like a cross between an angel and an alien, a being from another world. Her skin shimmered silver and her slim dress was an iridescent white. Her hair was laced with different types of large and lovely white flowers. She wore white stilettos.

Next Miguel emerged from another vehicle. He, too, was dressed completely in white: he wore a white tuxedo with a white bow tie and white shiny dress shoes. He looked stunning.

When Bee saw him she said, "Kakoi on krasavets! Ya tozhe vishla bi zamuzhem za nyevo."

"What?" whispered her mother in confusion.

The bride and groom walked together up the aisle to the stand in front of the guests. But what was strange was that there was no minister or priest. You could hear the buzz of people whispering and exchanging looks of surprise that said, "Where's the minister? Who's performing the ceremony?"

The wedding march ended and the musician announced, "Josephina and Miguel will now exchange vows."

And there they stood facing one another and holding onto one another's hands, in between those gathered and the calm surface of a lake.

Josephina began: I never told you this, but the night that I met you a voice came into my head and said, "This is going to be your husband." I thought I must be hallucinating, not only because I was high that evening, but because I didn't even know you, I had just met you for the first time. But now I realize the voice was right and strong hallucinations are sometimes visions of what is to be.

So, I promise that I will always be your friend. I will never desert you, even when I would rather run and hide; I will take your call; I will stand by your side. I will always strive to protect you from the negative energies that enter life's sphere and remind you that we have been given this life to love. If you should fall ill, I will care for you. If you should go insane, I will understand you. If you leave, I will never close the door to your return. I say all this because I vow to love you, not only through this life, but into the next.

In finishing her vows, Josephina bent her head down to Miguel's hands and kissed them.

Then Miguel spoke: Thank you. I cannot promise you that after this day I will never kiss another with passion. I cannot promise you that I will never be sexually intimate with another. I cannot promise you that you are the last person with whom I will fall in love. I cannot predict the future. But what I can promise you is that I will always be there for you and I will consider it the highest worldly honor if you will allow me the privilege of walking by your side down life's path. Our bond does not require legal agreements or contracts recognized by the state. Our souls are tethered in love and by god.

With this Miguel pulled a huge diamond ring from his pocket and placed it on Josephina's hand. It was clear from her surprised expression that she had never seen this ring before. She looked at it lovingly. Then she pulled a broad platinum band from the bosom of her dress and placed it on his finger, the two embraced, and kissed. The guests and the musician burst into happy applause.

The reception that followed was a picnic in the same park. One of Josephina's cousins was a professional caterer and she and her team put together an awesome picnic style meal of various sandwiches, pickles, macaroni and potato salads, wedding punch, etc. Everyone dined and relaxed on large white blankets with blue stars.

Towards the very end of the meal, everyone was quieted and Miguel's sister played and sang the bride and groom's song on an acoustic guitar; it was a song written by Tracy Loman called "Sweet." She sang sweetly, "We love one another, we trust one another. We like to just sit with each other, in peace. It's sweet." Many of the guests were brought to tears, including the bride and groom, their parents, and several aunts and uncles. As the attractive couple danced, a white swan with black eyes sailed peacefully by in the lake behind them. The guests quietly whispered and pointed at the animal, a marriage blessing from nature. Bee was reminded of someone she had met before.

After the first dance, Josephina announced that masks were being passed out and that every guest, without exception, was to don a mask, and join the bride and groom for the next dance. Miguel's sister joined forces with the keyboard player, a drummer, and a guy on maracas, and they were soon playing an energetic and upbeat salsa rhythm. Shortly thereafter all the guests were up and dancing. It looked wild to see everyone dancing in their masks! 'Twas a modern day masquerade ball; a wonderful party; a celebration of life.

As evening approached fewer people danced and more reclined, drinking, laughing, talking, thinking. And when the music stopped only one young person was still dancing. To those who noticed her, it almost appeared that she was dancing with someone else, an invisible partner, something in the way her eyes glowed or she would suddenly laugh or smile as if sharing some joke. Her mother watched her with tears of love in her eyes. Others enjoyed her, too. Some thought that she was out there, on some different plane of the same universe.

Miguel thought, "How beautiful she is! I would marry her, too."

As for Bee, a wave of peace washed over her as she danced there. This blissful feeling came to her: she was exactly who she needed to be.

ABOUT THE AUTHOR

Patricia Garcia lives in California. She loves reading and writing, singing and dancing to reggae music, and playing pai gow.

Patricia has been diagnosed with severe clinical depression. She is recovering through Buddhism, meditation, exercise, rest, and hydration.

Below is a picture of Styopa and the author when they lived in Russia as next door neighbors. You may read more about them in *Moscow in Slides.*

Visit Patricia Garcia's storefront at:
www.lulu.com/garcia

How do u want it?

www.ingramcontent.com/pod-product-compliance
Lightning Source LLC
Chambersburg PA
CBHW031852170626
46807CB00004B/1692